BECAUSE I FUCKING SAID SO

WRITTEN BY LIAM JAMES LEAVEN

ILLUSTRATED BY MARGARITA

All rights reserved. No part of this publication may be reproduced, distributed, stored in a retrieval system, or transmitted in any form, by any means, including mechanical, electronic, or by any other means, without the prior written permission of the author.

Copyright © 2024 Liam James Leaven

ISBN: 979-8-9904716-4-1

Étienne Editions, Virginia

ACKNOWLEDGMENTS

MY ETERNAL GRATITUDE TO MOM FOR YOUR UNWAVERING SUPPORT AND FOR RAISING US IN A HOME FILLED WITH LAUGHTER; TO NINOSKA, ISABEL AND ELLIE FOR YOUR BOUNDLESS LOVE AND HUMOR; AND TO EILEEN, FOR YOUR CONSISTENT ENCOURAGEMENT AND SHARP WIT—WE'LL LAUGH TOGETHER AGAIN ONE DAY. NONE OF THIS WOULD BE POSSIBLE WITHOUT THE LOVE, SUPPORT, AND LAUGHTER FROM ALL OF YOU.

—LJL

THIS BOOK BELONGS TO:

_____

(SOMEONE WHO IS VERY TIRED.
BUT WHO IS EVEN MORE LUCKY)

I used to play the game with you, my precious little one.

A thousand *whys* you'd always want to know.

But this game—you've won it!—There are no more answers to give.

So now to *why?* you'll only hear: because I fucking said so.

Sledding all morning on the season's first fallen snow, and now it's time to go in.

"But why?! Emma's allowed to stay. It's not fair!" you stomp, before throwing yourself in the snow.

Frostbite set in two hours ago. And I can't feel my face. (Is it still there?)

Because I fucking said so.

Running late for the school bus on a cold, windy day, and curiously,

it's always in special little moments like these when you have questions to pose, like:

"Why do I have to wear a coat, hat, shoes, or even pants?"

Wipe your snots. No more questions. Fuckin' said so.

Snack time is over, and you ask why you can't have one more.

"I promise, last one," begins your trademark 'just one more' lying promise manifesto.

Since your ultra-processed-food-compromised brain will have a total meltdown in the face of any rational response, let's try this:

I fuckin' said so.

Oh, precious darling, what a great day—I finally found that toy you've been begging me for!

You know—the limited-edition mystery surprise rainbow slime flamingo.

Say what? You wanted the *extra super rare* limited-edition mystery surprise rainbow slime flamingo? Well, you better fucking play with this piece of crap—and love it, forever. Why?

Because I ~~just paid five times retail for it on eBay~~ fucking said so.

Rolling on the dirty floor of the movie theatre in your own special, sweet way

because after a movie with popcorn, sour Nerds, Sprite, and gummy worms, to your request for ice cream, my answer was no.

Well, stay here overnight then—have fun with the monsters and zombies.

Just remember when they're eating your brains: I fuckin' told ya so.

"Why not just two more minutes, please please PLEASE!?" you cry, splashing sandy saltwater lovingly into my eyes

(scratching my cornea) as I get pulled into the undertow.

Listen closely to my air bubbles popping just above the surface, and you just might hear them—my last dying words:

because I fucking said so glub glub.

The afternoon begins so sweetly with a playful game of tag in the backyard,

but three hours in, when the 29th game has you just as exuberant as the first 28, and my blistered foot explodes like a volcano,

I'll wonder: Where's my wine?

Just leave me here to die. Go play on the slide. I fucking said so.

How do you make me so crazy,

when in my past—you should have seen it—I was so mellow!

But now I'm just a dumpster fire of failed internet parenting tips

and the expression that ends with "fucking said so."

"Chicken nuggets?" you inquire, as dinner arrives. "*Why* would you make me *that?*"

Are you trying to deal me the deathblow?

It's been your favorite food in the world every day for three years. You actually won't eat anything else, and we didn't have anymore at home, so today I left work early to get some, and I got yelled at by my boss because I'm always coming in late or leaving early because "the kids," and then I had to go to three stores because the first two didn't have the brand you like—*the blue one*—they only had the yellow one, which I knew you would throw on the floor in a fit, and this all made me 17 minutes late picking you up from daycare, so I had to pay an extra $85 at five dollars per minute, but you know what? I was actually thinking *no problem*, it's all worth it to make my little princess happy for dinnertime, but now . . .

Eat the nuggets. And these peas. I fucking said so.

Playing superheroes is fun until, inevitably, your adorable (but surprisingly solid) elbow careens into my face,

and you laugh—because you're a psycho.

If you jump on the couch one more time, you're dead.

Why? Fuckin' said so.

Of my former, single self, I am now just a shadow

as I hide in the bathroom incommunicado.

Oh privacy, my long-lost love, how I miss you dearly in these moments.

I'm pooping. Go see mommy. I fucking said so.

As bedtime approaches, and your tired eyes suddenly pop wide open with your endless wonder and play.

Another book, some water, more tickles, and answers to questions you want to know.

It's charming, I'll admit it. But you're not fooling me; it's just a ploy.

So out goes the light. Time to sleep. I fucking said so.

Yes, it's that old, familiar expression.

Ask your parents—surely, they'll know.

The one you swore you'd never say to your kids:

Because I fucking said so.

Liam James Leaven is the author of the comedic novel *On the Origins of Joy Boy's Chasm*, the parody book of motivational and inspirational mash-up quotes, *Huge Words by Huge People: Better Than Before*, and the comedic mash-up short of the Walton Letters in Mary Shelley's Frankenstein, *Frankenstein; or, the Modern Washingtonian*, which takes readers on an unforgettable romp through the Nevada deserts. He has two remarkable daughters who wouldn't be doing their job as kids if they didn't, from time to time, make him ponder that old, familiar expression. Get on the bus at liamjamesleaven.com to join him on his uproarious and insightful quest for hijinks.

Margarita is a Ukrainian illustrator whose artistry shines through in her use of color and form, creating memorable illustrations with striking visual compositions. Her work has appeared in children's books, graphic novels, and books of poetry in collaboration with authors across Ukraine and internationally from Italy, Germany, Bulgaria, the United Kingdom, and the United States.

Made in the USA
Middletown, DE
20 September 2024